W9-BNI-569

Rescue Me

Maurice's Lucky Day

Story by
Eleanor Turino

Illustrations by
F. Gonmuki

Thanks to all my literary friends:

Ramona, Amos, Boris, Corduroy, Wilbur, Charlotte, Amaroq, Julie, Ferdinand, Matilda, Junie B, Max, Amelia, Frog and Toad, Madeline, Dick, Jane, Nancy D, Ping, Sam, Bangs, Moonshine, Gooney Bird, Trixie, Pigeon, Mike Mulligan, Mary Ann, Frederick, Swimmy, Winnie, Anne with an "e", Pippi and many more.

Maurice the library book did not like being in the library. He disliked the quiet and the stillness on weekends without children and most of all he missed being read.

Now the library would be closed for winter vacation. If he didn't get picked today he would be stuck on his shelf for a week without being read and shared. Fortunately, Maurice was picked and he was headed to the airport with a boy and his family for a vacation.

"This is my lucky day," he said.

It was Maurice's first flight. He was thrilled. Maurice was being read by two brothers. They only looked up when the flight attendant came by with a cart load of snacks.

The plane landed and a gangway was rolled up to the door. Maurice felt a gentle breeze and the warmth of the tropical sun on his cover. He'd read books about tropical paradises but never dreamed he would see one.

Once the family reached their hotel, they unpacked and set out for the beach. The excitement of traveling left Maurice exhausted.

In the evening the brothers took turns reading Maurice, late into the night.

The next morning Maurice relaxed by the pool in the shade of an umbrella. The umbrella shielded Maurice from a surprise shower of bird poop! Unfortunately not everyone was covered.

After a day of relaxing, the family toured the island by bike.

Another day, the family signed up for scuba diving lessons. Maurice decided to go to the gift shop instead.

The week passed quickly. The flight home was scheduled for early in the morning. Unfortunately, everyone over slept. They packed frantically.

They checked the drawers, closets and under the beds. Everything was packed - except for Maurice. He was asleep in the tangled sheets.

When Maurice woke up, he was alone. He was startled by a knock at the door. A voice called out, "housekeeping". Maurice couldn't move in the tangled sheets.

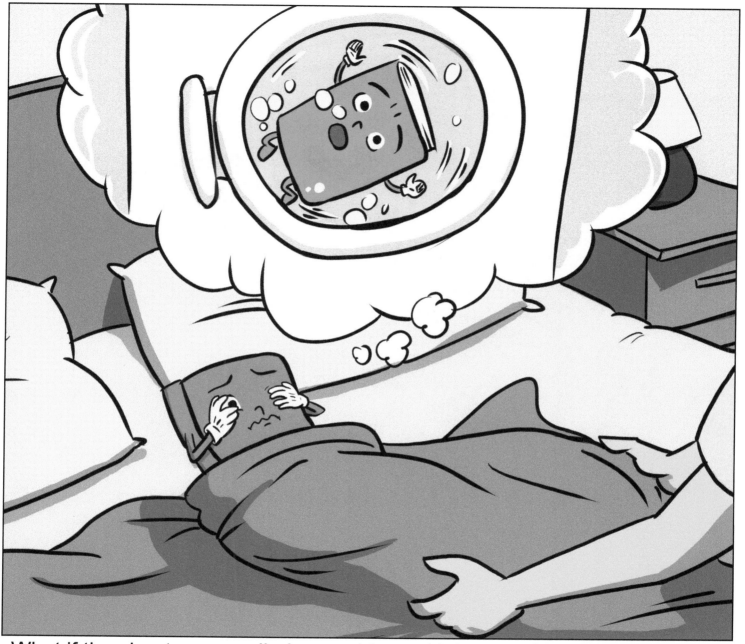

What if the sheets were rolled up and tossed into a washing machine? "Rescue me! Please rescue me." The sheets were pulled back. A hand reached out and gently lifted him. "Did someone just rescue me?"

It was a young woman. She placed him on her cleaning cart. Maurice waited as the woman went from room to room.

Hours later, she plucked Maurice from the cart, walked to the employee locker room and put him in her tote bag. "Where am I going?", he wondered.

They walked to a grand building with a long, wide staircase. Maurice gasped as he entered the building.

Books were everywhere - stacked in piles on tables, high up on balcony shelves with ladders to reach them, and books on walls from floor to ceiling. This must be a public library!

The young woman walked to the librarian's desk. They spoke.
Maurice was handed to the librarian and the two women said goodbye.

The librarian addressed a manila envelope, wrote a note and gently
slipped Maurice and the note into the envelope. "Where am I going?", he
asked himself.

(He was being mailed.)

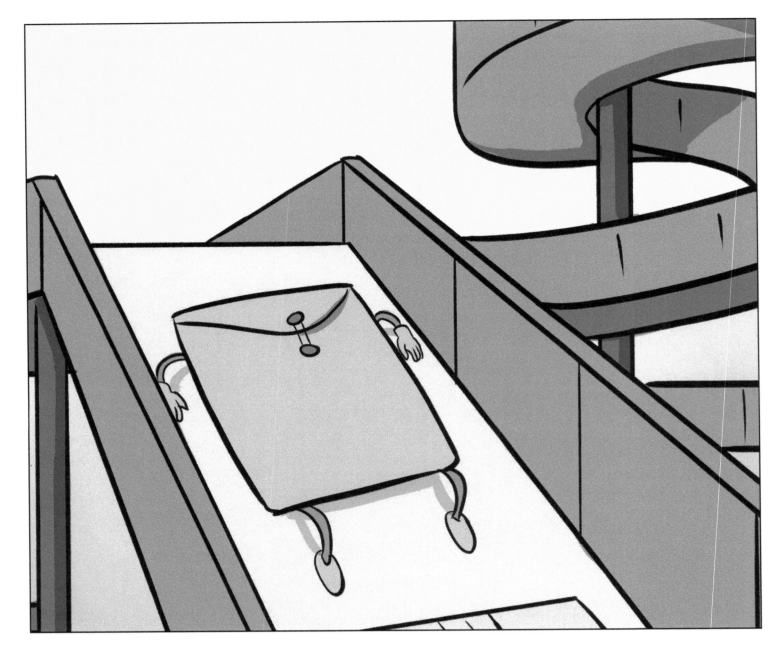

In the morning, Maurice was in a post office. He was stamped, weighed and tossed onto a long chute. He was scanned by red lights and measured with beams of blue lights on his front end and back end.

A bed of metal rollers came next. After all the sorting, shifting and rolling Maurice had travelled the length of a football field! He was going to be loaded into the belly of an airplane. Would he ever make it back to his library shelf? "Rescue me. Please rescue me!"

The next thing he knew, he was on a postal delivery route. The mail carrier entered a building. Maurice heard voices, laughter and the faint sound of a bell. These sounds were familiar to him.

The mail carrier reached an office. Maurice's envelope was placed on the edge of a desk. When the mail carrier left the room the door slammed. The sound startled Maurice and he fell from the edge of the desk into a nearby trash bin. He clung to the rim of the bin with all his might. As he was about to lose his grip, a hand reached out and lifted him to safety. "I think someone just rescued me!" Maurice breathed a sigh of relief.

His envelope was opened. There was a familiar library face looking at him.
It was Mrs. Cap, the library clerk. She was shocked to see Maurice. Maurice
was shocked to see her. He'd been missing for weeks.

"He's back!" exclaimed Mrs.Cap. She read the note attached to Maurice's front cover. *"This book was left in a hotel room and was returned to our public library. We hope the book made its way home. Sincerely....".* She checked Maurice for signs of damage. He was in excellent condition.

Maurice was lovingly returned to his place on the library shelf.

Once he was settled, he nudged his neighbor and said,
"**This** is my lucky day!"

The End.

Author's Note

This story is based on an actual event. Several years ago, just before the winter break, a student borrowed a school library book and brought it on vacation to Disney World, Florida.

Several weeks later I received a large manila envelope addressed to the school library. Inside, there was a library book with a short note attached explaining that the book was left in a hotel room. It was brought to the local public library and in turn, returned to our school. This event provided the seed of an idea which grew into the story, **Rescue Me: Maurice's Lucky Day**.

CPSIA information can be obtained
at www.ICGtesting.com
Printed in the USA
BVHW022326110119
537672BV00004B/78/P